NEVER T[OO] LITTLE TO HELP

Written by Diane C. Ohanesian
Illustrated by Scott Ross

Copyright © MCMXCII Playmore Inc., Publishers
and Waldman Publishing Corp., New York, New York
All rights reserved
Printed in China

Peter's family was very busy, getting ready for their vacation. Peter was very excited. He loved vacations. He wanted to help too.

Peter tried to help his big sister Amy carry her suitcase to the car.

"I'm big enough to do this by myself, Peter," Amy said.

"Dad's in the garage. Go and see if he needs help."

Whoosh! Peter ran through the house as fast as he could. Maybe Dad really needs my help, he thought.

The garage was full. Suitcases and boxes, rafts and bikes and boats and floats were scattered everywhere. Dad had many things to load into the car.

Peter saw a small suitcase, just the size for him to carry. Maybe all my things are in there, Peter thought. We wouldn't want to leave without that! I'll help Dad put it in the car.

"Whoa!" said Dad as Peter lifted the suitcase towards the trunk. "There's so much that must go in, I haven't figured it out yet. Why don't you go and see if Mom needs any help?"

That was a good idea. Mom always had things for Peter to help with. She must be really busy now.

As Peter peeked into the laundry room, he heard a loud whirrump. . .whirrump. . . whirrumping sound. Mom was doing some last minute laundry.

Now this was a job for Peter! He always liked helping Mom take and fold the things that were warm and fresh and snuggly from the dryer. Now he could help!

"Oh, Peter," said Mom. "You're my best helper. But today, I really must do this by myself. Some of these towels and clothes are to be put away, and some are for our trip. I must think which are which. Why don't you go outside and play until it's time for us to leave?"

Poor Peter! He wanted to help everybody but nobody seemed to need him. He wanted to get everything ready so vacation could start soon. But all he could do was go out and play while everyone else in the family did the work. He walked sadly toward his play tent in the yard.

That was where he kept some of his favorite toys. Peter had a little telescope for star hunting, a flashlight for night animal hunting, and a glass jar for catching lightning bugs.

While Peter played in the tent, Mom, Dad, and Amy had finished packing. Now they would all start their vacation! Peter raced out of the tent and into the house.

When they went out to the car, it was so packed with boxes and cases and bags and things, Peter wondered if there was room enough for him! But of course there was. And they all piled in.

"Wait a minute," cried Amy as she fastened her seatbelt. "Where's Penny?" The little puppy that had been underfoot all day was nowhere to be seen! They called and whistled for the puppy, but Penny didn't come running in the way she usually did

Amy ran into the house to find the missing puppy.
After a long wait, she came back to the car.

"I can't find Penny anywhere," she said.

Then the whole family went puppy hunting. Dad searched the basement for some of Penny's favorite sleeping places—inside an old wheelbarrow, atop a pile of blankets, underneath a big wooden desk. No Penny!

Mom searched under the beds, behind the livingroom sofa, even inside the kitchen cabinets. Still no Penny.

"Penny!" Amy called as she crawled around the plastic swimming pool and under the slide of the swing set. "Penny, where are you?" But no Penny.

Peter watched as they looked here, there, and everywhere for the puppy. Suddenly, he had an idea.

Peter ran to his room. Toys and stuff were scattered everywhere. There were things all over the floor. But Peter knew he hadn't made that mess!

He opened the door to his closet and uncovered his secret hiding place. There, right on top of his special stuff was Penny! She had scattered everything around to make herself a bed and was sleeping quietly while the whole family was rushing about looking for her!

Peter scooped up the sleeping puppy and carried her to the car.

"You found her!" cried Amy.

"Good job, Peter," said Dad.

"You're still the best helper, Peter!" Mom smiled proudly.

Now at last they could start their vacation—Mom, Dad, Amy, and Peter, who knew for sure you're never too little to help!